THE MARONITES OF LEBANON

Identity Crisis, A Divided Nation

DR. ABRAHAM KHOUREIS, Ph.D.

Copyright Notice

Note & Disclaimer

This book is a fictional work of literature inspired by true events. While it draws from historical accounts, traditions, and collective memory, certain characters, dialogues, and scenes have been adapted for narrative purposes. Although it is based on accurate historical resources, it is not intended to serve as a definitive historical record.

Any resemblance to actual persons, living or deceased, as well as to organizations, institutions, governments, or groups, beyond the well-known historical figures and entities referenced, is entirely coincidental and unintentional.

The purpose of this work is to honor the essence of events and to explore their moral, spiritual, and human significance through the medium of authentic and real storytelling.

Lebanon: People and Cultures Series

Lebanon is more than a point on the Mediterranean map; it is a living mosaic of peoples, faiths, and traditions whose encounters, conflicts, and sacrifices have shaped its destiny.

In this honest and thoughtful series, Dr. Abraham Khoureis, Ph.D., a global thinker, leadership scholar, and apostle of compassionate leadership examines Lebanon's communities with clarity and courage, bringing their histories and identities to light.

Each volume explores both the triumphs and the trials of this diverse land:

The Shia of Lebanon: The Guardians of the Nation, celebrating endurance, sacrifice, and their vital role in defending Lebanon's sovereignty.

The Druze of Lebanon: Keepers of the Mountain, unveiling the resilience and spiritual uniqueness of this mountain community.

The Maronites of Lebanon: Identity Crisis, A Divided Nation, confronting the legacy of power and imbalance while recognizing their contributions and underserved privilege.

The Sunnis of Lebanon: Between Coast and Power, tracing their influence in Lebanon's coastal cities and their links to the wider Arab world.

Future volumes will bring forward the stories of Lebanon's other communities.

Together, these works form a comprehensive account of Lebanon's people and cultures, a portrait both unflinching and compassionate. They speak to leaders, scholars, and citizens alike, reminding the world that Lebanon cannot be understood without acknowledging all its communities.

It is written with the hope that the insights within these pages will guide those in power to safeguard this fragile, divided country, so that Lebanon may yet rediscover unity, dignity, and peace.

Table of Contents

"There can be no country or dignity without unity of the people, and there can be no unity without agreement..."

Rene Moawad

Preface

Lebanon has always been a land of contrasts, perched at the meeting point of East and West, of mountains and sea, of survival and collapse. It is a country whose history is both magnificent and tragic, and within it, each community has played a role in shaping the destiny of the nation. Among these communities, the Maronites stand out for their resilience, their ambitions, their foreign and regional alliances, and their controversies.

This book is a testimony of history as it unfolded, written to strip away illusions and tell the truth as it can be verified. The Maronites are often described as the community that carried Lebanon on its shoulders, building schools, hospitals, and banks, claiming Phoenician ancestry, and presenting themselves as the guardians of a Christian presence in the Middle East. Yet history tells a more complex story: one of privilege, dependence on foreign powers, internal divisions, and repeated betrayals, sometimes of others, often of themselves.

The pages that follow trace their origins, their settlement in the mountains of Lebanon, and the way they shaped and reshaped their identity over the centuries. We will see how they allied with Crusaders, leaned on France, welcomed European influence, and later, how they interacted with Israel and America. We will examine how these choices brought them temporary privilege but left them weakened when foreign patrons shifted their priorities. We will explore their role in shaping Lebanon's political system, their contribution to culture and education, their involvement in wars and conflicts, and their place in the collapse of the modern Lebanese state.

The narrative does not aim to single out one sect for blame in a land where all have played their part in division. Rather, it seeks to hold a reminder to the Maronite experience, because only by confronting truth can a community grow beyond it. Their history reveals lessons that matter not only for Lebanon, but for every people who wrestle with identity, privilege, and belonging in a world that constantly tempts them to lean on outsiders rather than trust their own.

What follows is an account of a community that was given much, that achieved much, but that also lost much through arrogance, illusion, and disunity. It is also the story of what might still be redeemed, if humility and loyalty to the land are embraced over pride and denial.

This book is written with the conviction that truth, however difficult, is more valuable than illusion, however comforting. It is offered as an act of record, so that future generations may know what was done, what was lost, and what remains possible.

Introduction

Lebanon is a small land, yet its people often carry ambitions far larger than its mountains and valleys can contain. Every community has told a story of itself, a story that explains why it matters, why it deserves a voice, and why its place is indispensable to the nation. The Maronites have been among the most persistent in this exercise of self-definition, and their story has shaped Lebanon's past more than most. To understand Lebanon, one must understand them.

The Maronites trace their origins to a small community of Christians who followed Saint Maron in the region of Syria during the early centuries of Christianity. Over time, they moved into the mountains of Lebanon, carving out villages and monasteries in the highlands where rugged terrain offered protection. This move was not 2,000 years ago, as some later claimed, but centuries afterward, well after Christianity's birth. Their migration was a pragmatic retreat to the mountains where survival was possible.

With time, they wrapped themselves in myths. The claim of Phoenician descent became a central narrative, meant to distinguish them from their Arab and Muslim neighbors and even from other Christians. To be Phoenician was to claim a lineage that predated both Christianity and Islam, to link oneself to a seafaring people who traded with the ancient world, who built Tyre and Byblos, who once carried civilization across the Mediterranean. But history offers little evidence of such continuity. Their language was Arabic, their culture woven into the Arab world, their faith shaped by the broader Christian East. The Phoenician story was an illusion, an identity crisis of belonging, a political move and a way to align with the West, to carve out a claim of difference. They created their own identity crisis.

This narrative of difference guided their path for centuries. When Crusaders came through the Levant, Maronite leaders found in them not invaders but potential allies. Later, France became their patron, offering protection and privilege in exchange for loyalty. When the Ottoman Empire collapsed after the First World War, it was France that carved Greater Lebanon and granted the Maronites the presidency, a privilege unmatched by numbers. Their schools, hospitals, and banking system were hailed as proof of advancement, yet much of it was built with Western assistance and modeled after European systems, designed as much for foreign elites as for Lebanese citizens.

This privilege carried consequences. When Israel invaded Lebanon, some Maronite leaders aligned themselves with it, believing that foreign arms would secure their dominance. When American influence grew in the region, Maronite parties often became its willing partners, reinforcing the perception that their survival depended on Western backing rather than national unity. The collapse of Lebanon's banking system in the twenty-first century further exposed the fragility of this model. For years, the central bank under Riad Salameh, a

Maronite, operated on financial engineering that became indistinguishable from a Ponzi scheme. The rich and well-connected, many from Lebanon's traditional families, benefited. Ordinary citizens, of all sects, lost their savings, their dignity, and their trust.

The Maronites were not the only sect responsible for Lebanon's corruption, but as the community long presented as the "face" of Lebanon, they carried a heavy share of blame. Their story is not just of resilience and survival; it is of privilege that excluded, ambition that overreached, and alliances that betrayed.

This book tells that story with clarity and without apology. It will explore their origins, their myths, their alliances with Crusaders and colonial powers, their role in shaping Lebanon's political system, their involvement in civil war, their place in the modern financial collapse, and finally, their dwindling numbers and uncertain future. It will examine how a community that once seemed to embody Lebanon's promise came to embody many of its failures.

But it will also look forward. For as their power drains and their numbers fall, the Maronites face a choice. They can cling to myths and foreign patrons, repeating the arrogance of the past, or they can embrace humility, unity, and loyalty to Lebanon. Their fate will not be decided in Paris or Washington, nor in ancient myths of Phoenicians, but in their ability to stand beside Shia, Sunni, Druze, and all others as partners in rebuilding a nation that has long been broken.

The story of the Maronites is, in many ways, the story of Lebanon itself: grand in ambition, tragic in collapse, and still uncertain in its outcome. To study them is not to single them out for blame but to hold up a reminder to a nation that has too often betrayed itself.

Where did the Maronites Come From?

Every people has a beginning, and the Maronites are no exception. Long before they made the mountains of Lebanon their stronghold, their story took shape on the hills of northern Syria, where a monk named Maron chose to live a life unlike any other.

Maron lived near Cyrrhus, not far from Antioch, at the end of the fourth and start of the fifth century. He was known for his extreme simplicity. He did not seek the shelter of a roof or the comfort of a cell. Instead, he lived under the open sky, exposed to heat and cold, devoting his days and nights to prayer. His life of discipline and faith drew people to him. Some came for guidance, others to be healed in body or spirit. Many stayed, becoming his disciples and carrying his way of life forward.

We know about Maron because Theodoret, the bishop of Cyrrhus, wrote about him not long after his death. Theodoret described Maron as a man whose soul was filled with God's grace. He told how Maron turned a ruined pagan temple into a place of prayer, and how his presence brought strength to those who were weary or sick. These words matter because they are the earliest record we have, showing that Maron was remembered in his own time as a man of holiness and influence.

After his death, Monk Maron's followers built communities that combined prayer with daily work. Over time, these communities grew into monasteries. The greatest of them was the Monastery of Saint Maron, standing on the banks of the Orontes River in what was then called Syria Secunda. By the sixth century, this monastery had become famous across the region. In 518, the pope in Rome even referred to the monks of Saint Maron in his letters, proof that their reputation had spread far beyond their homeland.

This land, the Orontes valley and the hills around it, was the first home of the Maronites. Here they prayed in Syriac, a form of Aramaic, and followed the Antiochene school of Christian teaching. That tradition stressed both the humanity and the divinity of Christ, holding them together without confusion. When the Council of Chalcedon met in 451 and fierce arguments split the Christian world, the followers of Maron were known for their loyalty to the Chalcedonian faith. That loyalty became one of the marks of their identity.

But history soon changed their path. In the seventh century, new theological struggles unsettled the empire. In the middle of these upheavals, many of the Maronites began to leave their Syrian homeland. They moved west and south, toward the mountains of Lebanon. The steep valleys and high ridges gave them a refuge, both from imperial officials and from new rulers. In those mountains, their way of life endured.

By the ninth century, the Maronites were firmly settled in Lebanon. The mountains became their lasting home, but they never forgot where they had come from. Their first homeland lay farther north, near Cyrrhus and the Orontes River, where a humble monk had prayed under the open sky, where his monastery stood, and where their faith and identity first took root. Lebanon was their second chapter, born out of hardship and necessity, but also out of resilience. Their beginnings, however, were originated and written on the hills of Syria.

From Antioch to the Mountains

Antioch was one of the great centers of Christianity, and from it radiated churches, liturgies, and schools of thought that would shape much of the Eastern tradition. The Maronites were born in this world, part of the Syriac Christian family, speaking Syriac as their liturgical language and sharing much with other communities of the Levant.

Their early centuries were not easy. Theological disputes that split Christendom often placed them at odds with larger churches. At one point, their adherence to certain Christological positions led to their isolation from both Rome and Constantinople, though centuries later they would reestablish communion with the Roman Catholic Church. For survival, they learned the art of persistence, remaining small but united, vulnerable yet determined to endure.

By the early Middle Ages, their circumstances forced them to move. Pressures from stronger empires, political instability, and the desire for a defensible homeland pushed many of them southward into the mountains of Lebanon. These mountains, rugged and often inaccessible, became their fortress. Valleys and ridges that seemed inhospitable to outsiders offered safety to a people determined to survive without being absorbed. It was in these mountains that the Maronites began to form the identity that would define them for centuries.

Their migration was not an unbroken chain stretching back two thousand years, as some later claimed. It was not a direct inheritance from the Phoenicians, who had long vanished as a distinct people. Rather, it was the pragmatic choice of a small Christian community seeking safety in a world where survival often depended on the ability to retreat. The mountains of Lebanon gave them that chance.

Here, the Maronites supported by France, outside missionary Christian groups, and western powers had built villages, churches, and monasteries. They tilled the rocky soil, raised goats, and relied on the strength of kinship ties to bind their settlements together. Their life was hard, but it gave them something far more valuable than wealth: independence. In the mountains, they could preserve their faith, their language of worship, and their internal cohesion. Over time, this created a fierce sense of identity, one that combined humility in daily survival with pride in having endured where others had been scattered.

It was also in these mountains that their mythologies began to grow. Surrounded by Arab Muslims, Druze, and other Christian sects, the Maronites sought to distinguish themselves. By the nineteenth century, some of their intellectuals and leaders began to falsely claim that they were descendants of the Phoenicians, the ancient seafarers of the Levant. To be Phoenician was to say, "We are not Arab, we are older, we are distinct." This claim served a political purpose more than a historical one. It was a way to appeal to European powers who romanticized the

Phoenicians as the ancestors of Mediterranean trade and civilization. It was also a way to justify privilege within Lebanon, to argue that they were the original people of the land. Yet the truth remained: their origins lay not in the mythical Phoenicians but in the Christian monastic movements of Syria, later transplanted into Lebanon's mountains. Their language was Arabic, their culture intertwined with the Arab world, and their fate inseparable from it.

This duality, of fact and myth, would mark the Maronites throughout history. On one hand, they were a mountain people, hardy and rooted, clinging to survival in stone villages and monasteries. On the other, they claimed a heritage that elevated them above their neighbors, seeking legitimacy not only from the land but from distant ancestors and powerful foreign allies. This tension between reality and aspiration would shape their politics, their alliances, and their eventual role in the making of modern Lebanon.

In these early centuries, what defined the Maronites most was not wealth or power, but endurance. The mountains were not a place of privilege, but of hardship. Yet from hardship came resilience. This resilience would later serve them well, but it would also tempt them into overreach when new patrons offered them privilege beyond their numbers. The seeds of both their survival and their eventual struggles were planted in these rugged valleys, when a small Christian community chose the mountains of Lebanon as its home.

The Illusions of Phoenician Ancestry

In the late part of the twentieth century many Maronite writers and politicians, illusionist by the undeserved privilege and outer-hate toward their environment and neighbors falsely claimed descent from the ancient Phoenicians, presenting themselves as heirs of a seafaring civilization that once traded across the Mediterranean. This story was not innocent. It was used to craft an identity separate from the Arabs around them, an identity that tied them to Europe rather than to the East. In schoolbooks, in speeches, and in monuments, the

17

Phoenician story became a banner of Maronite pride.

But the verified history does not support the myth. The Phoenicians lived on the Levantine coast more than two thousand years before the Maronites ever appeared and existed. Their language, culture, and cities faded into history long before Christianity, let alone the Maronite Church, was born in Syria. No continuous line connects the mountain villagers of the early Maronites to the traders of Tyre and Sidon. What does connect them is the land itself, but the people who lived on that land changed many times over.

Serious historians such as Kamal Salibi, a Christian, have pointed out that the Phoenician claim was less about ancestry and more about politics. Under the French Mandate, the myth served a purpose: it gave the Maronites a story that set them apart from their Arab and Muslim neighbors, making them seem older, more Western, and more entitled to lead the new state. The French encouraged this idea, for it justified their creation of Greater Lebanon as a

Christian-led enclave. What was presented as history was, in fact, a colonial false narrative, and the Maronites believed it intentionally, or otherwise. An identity crisis that later divided a nation.

The truth is simpler and harder to deny. The Maronites spoke Arabic, prayed in Syriac, and lived as part of the Arab world. They were not Phoenicians, and they were not Europeans. They were children of the Levant, originated in Syria and formed by the mountains of Lebanon and the currents of the Arab East. Their survival was real, but their claim to antiquity was false and manufactured. By clinging to this myth, they distanced themselves from their neighbors and betrayed their own real identity.

Settlement and Identity

When the Maronites settled in the mountains of Lebanon, they did more than find refuge; they began to craft an identity. These mountains, rugged and resistant to conquest, became the crucible in which their sense of self was forged. Unlike communities that thrived in fertile plains or bustling cities, the Maronites survived by endurance rather than abundance. Their villages clung to terraced hillsides, their monasteries were hewn into cliffs, and their lives were defined by labor, prayer, and kinship. In this environment, identity was not an abstract notion, it was the very condition of survival.

The isolation of the mountains gave them both strength and vulnerability. Cut off from the larger currents of the empire and trade, they developed an inward-looking character, bound tightly by family and parish. The church became the anchor of community life, not only in spiritual matters but also in governance and social order. Bishops and priests often acted as mediators, judges, and leaders, guiding a people who relied on their cohesion to endure external pressures. Over time, this produced a close bond between religious authority and communal identity, making the Maronite Church inseparable from the Maronite people.

The Maronites were never completely alone. Their mountain settlements sat beside Druze villages, Shia and Sunni Muslim communities, and other Christian sects. Relations with neighbors were often tense, marked by competition over land, water, and influence. At times, conflict erupted into open hostility; at others, pragmatic alliances allowed coexistence. This rhythm of rivalry and accommodation became another feature of Maronite identity: the constant need to assert distinctiveness while negotiating survival among others.

In shaping their identity, the Maronites drew deeply from the church. Liturgies in Syriac linked them to their origins near Antioch, even as daily life was lived in Arabic. Their theology was rooted in Eastern Christianity, yet their renewed communion with

Rome gave them a bridge to the West. This dual belonging, Eastern in origin, Western in aspiration, became central to their sense of who they were. They were Arabs in language and culture, yet they insisted on being more than Arab; they were Eastern Christians tied to Rome, yet distinct from European Catholics. This layered identity gave them flexibility, but it also built contradictions that would later strain their politics.

By the time of the Ottoman Empire, the Maronites had grown in number and influence, concentrated in Mount Lebanon but spread across other regions as well. The Ottomans recognized them as part of the millet system, allowing them autonomy in religious matters but binding them to imperial authority. Within this structure, Maronite leaders learned how to maneuver, to pay taxes, to negotiate privileges, to appeal to foreign powers when useful. Identity here was not just about faith or heritage; it was about learning how to survive as a minority under shifting empires.

It was during this period that the myths of Phoenician ancestry began to crystallize more fully. The Maronites, seeking to elevate themselves above their Muslim neighbors and secure favor with European powers, began to emphasize their supposed descent from the ancient seafarers of the Levant. To call themselves Phoenician was to claim antiquity, distinction, and a tie to the Mediterranean world rather than to the Arab one. The idea was appealing to European patrons who romanticized the Phoenicians, and it gave the Maronites a narrative of uniqueness. But as historians later confirmed, it was more invention than reality, a myth carefully cultivated to serve political ends.

This mythmaking reveals something deeper about Maronite identity: it was always a negotiation between reality and aspiration. In reality, they were a mountain people, Arabic-speaking and bound to the fate of the Levant. In aspiration, they were heirs to Phoenicians, allies of Crusaders, partners of Europeans, and guardians of a Christian Lebanon. These two layers never fully aligned, and the gap between them often created tensions both within the community and with others.

By the dawn of the modern era, the Maronites had established themselves as a distinct and recognized community, one that combined religious devotion, cultural resilience, and political ambition. Their settlements in Mount Lebanon were no longer just refuges, they were centers of identity, projecting a narrative of endurance and uniqueness. The mountains had given them survival, but identity gave them a story. And in Lebanon, stories often mattered as much as armies.

It was this story of difference, rooted in survival but amplified by myth, that would later propel the Maronites into positions of privilege. But the very myths that gave them leverage would also sow the seeds of their disunity and decline, for no community can live forever on illusions without confronting the truth beneath them.

The Mountain Refuge

For centuries, the mountains of Lebanon were more than geography; they were the heartbeat of Maronite survival. The steep ridges, narrow valleys, and inaccessible highlands offered protection that no empire could fully penetrate. To outsiders, Mount Lebanon was harsh, rocky, and poor in resources. To the Maronites, it was freedom.

Life in the mountain was hard. The soil was thin, the winters cold, and the roads often impassable. Families survived by farming terraced plots, tending olive trees, pressing grapes, and raising goats. Their wealth was never in gold or vast estates, but in their endurance and their ability to cling to land that outsiders found too difficult to tame. Out of this hardship came a fierce independence, a sense that they alone could endure what others could not. It gave them pride, but it also reinforced their insularity.

The monasteries scattered across the mountains became more than places of prayer. They were centers of community, of teaching, and of administration. The church, inseparable from the people, became their leader in both spirit and governance. Priests mediated disputes, monks managed lands, and bishops guided communal affairs. The Maronite patriarch, often sheltered in mountain monasteries, became the symbolic head of the community, embodying both religious authority and political representation. This union of church and people gave the Maronites cohesion but also made their identity heavily dependent on clerical leadership.

The mountains also gave them a refuge from the shifting storms of empire. The Byzantines, the Arabs, and later the Ottomans controlled the plains, the cities, and the trade routes. But the mountains remained stubbornly difficult to dominate. Empires taxed and sometimes raided the Maronites, but rarely could they impose lasting control. This semi-independence gave the Maronites space to breathe, but it also kept them on the margins of economic life. They were safe, but they were poor, bound to the rhythm of subsistence living.

It was in this refuge that the Maronites developed their sense of exceptionalism. They saw themselves as a chosen community, preserved by God in the mountains while others bent to empire. Their liturgies in Syriac tied them to ancient Christianity, while their survival in Lebanon reinforced the belief that they were guardians of a unique destiny. Over time, this sense of closeness hardened into a conviction of difference, a belief that they were not merely one community among many but something set apart.

But the mountains also taught them the value of alliances. Though isolated, they were not entirely alone. They traded with coastal towns, negotiated with Druze and Muslim neighbors, and sometimes allied with stronger powers to secure their position. This dual posture, proud independence within, pragmatic alliance without, became a defining feature of Maronite politics. They could retreat into the mountains when threatened, but they also knew when to reach outward for protection and support.

The mountain refuge preserved them, but it also

shaped their worldview. It gave them resilience but raised the suspicion of outsiders. It gave them identity but encouraged mythmaking about their origins. It gave them protection but limited their participation in broader economic and political life. Above all, it instilled in them the belief that survival required both unity within and alliances beyond.

As the centuries passed, the Maronites would emerge from their mountain strongholds to play larger roles in Lebanon and the region. Yet the imprint of the mountains never left them. Even when they gained privilege, their political instincts were still those of a mountain people: wary, defensive, dependent on patrons, and proud of endurance. The refuge of Mount Lebanon had saved them, but it also confined them, a paradox that would echo through every chapter of their later history.

Relations with Neighbors

The mountains of Lebanon were never inhabited by the Maronites alone. From the very beginning, their villages and monasteries existed alongside Druze strongholds, Shia farming communities, Sunni coastal towns, and other Christian sects. Lebanon was never a land of one people but a patchwork, and this patchwork forced the Maronites into constant negotiation.

Relations with the Druze were perhaps the most defining. The Druze, themselves a mountain community, shared the rugged terrain with the Maronites and often clashed with them over land, water, and political control. At times, fierce battles erupted, leaving scars that lasted generations. Yet at other times, the two communities found ways to coexist, even to form temporary alliances when outside powers threatened them both. The rhythm was never stable, war one decade, partnership the next, but it ensured that neither Druze nor Maronites could claim the mountain as theirs alone.

Relations with the Shia of the south and the Beqaa were marked by distance more than intimacy. The Shia were farmers tied to the plains, while the Maronites were villagers of the highlands. Their worlds rarely overlapped directly, but they were linked by the wider currents of power. Both communities were often marginalized by empires, both relied on resilience for survival, but their trajectories diverged. Where the Maronites sought European patronage, the Shia remained rooted in their lands and tied to clerical traditions that gave them endurance without privilege. This difference, one community lifted by outsiders, the other ignored, would shape Lebanon's politics in ways that became painfully visible in the modern era.

Relations with Sunnis were more complex still. The Sunnis, concentrated in coastal cities like Tripoli, Sidon, and Beirut, were part of the Ottoman ruling elite. They controlled trade, ports, and much of the wealth. The Maronites, mountain-bound and dependent on subsistence, looked to them with a mixture of envy and resentment. When European influence grew, it was often the Maronites who became its local beneficiaries, while Sunnis saw their primacy challenged. This created rivalries that played out not only in politics but also in identity, Sunnis framing themselves as heirs of empire, Maronites presenting themselves as heirs of Phoenicians and as protégés of the West.

Even within Christianity, relations were fraught. The Greek Orthodox, larger in number and rooted in coastal towns, often viewed the Maronites as upstarts who exaggerated their role. Other smaller Christian sects sometimes resented the Maronites' alignment with Rome and their claims of superiority. Yet in times of crisis, Christians often leaned on one another, if only to survive in a land dominated by larger Muslim communities.

This mosaic of neighbors gave Lebanon its richness but also its fragility. No community was strong enough to dominate on its own, yet each sought to carve a privileged place. For the Maronites, relations with neighbors were always a balance between assertion and dependence. They fought when they believed they could prevail, but they also sought alliances when the threat was too great. They knew they could not live alone, but they never stopped trying to present themselves as different, as special, as destined for more.

These patterns of tension and accommodation became the foundation of Lebanon's sectarian system. The Maronites' relations with Druze, Shia, Sunnis, and other Christians would shape not just local disputes but the very structure of the nation that later emerged. For in Lebanon, neighbors were never just neighbors; they were competitors, allies, rivals, and partners all at once. And for the Maronites, navigating this fragile web was both their necessity and, eventually, their undoing.

From Ottoman Rule to Collapse

When the Ottoman Empire absorbed the Levant in the sixteenth century, the Maronites became one of many minority communities under the Sultan's rule. The empire governed through the millet system, which allowed religious communities autonomy in their spiritual and internal affairs so long as they paid taxes and acknowledged Ottoman authority. For the Maronites, this meant survival without full equality. They could worship, they could preserve their church, but they were subject to the will of the empire and the intermediaries it appointed.

Life under Ottoman rule was not uniform. In Mount Lebanon, local emirs held sway, mediating between the Maronite villages and the imperial administration. The most notable of these were the Shihab and Ma'an dynasties, which balanced Druze, Maronite, and Muslim interests while keeping Ottoman oversight at bay. For the Maronites, this arrangement was tolerable: they were not crushed, but neither were they dominant. They remained a mountain people, taxed but largely left to govern their own affairs.

Over time, however, they sought ways to elevate their position. The Maronite Church, through its patriarchs, began to strengthen ties with Rome, reaffirming its communion with the Catholic Church and seeking recognition as the Eastern guardians of Christianity. This connection gave them leverage, for Rome's blessing made them more than just another mountain sect, it made them a Christian bridge to Europe. The French, in particular, embraced this role. By the seventeenth century, France had declared itself the protector of Catholics in the Ottoman Empire, and the Maronites benefited most from this arrangement.

This protection was both a blessing and a trap. It gave them advantages, access to education, trade networks, and political influence that other communities lacked. Maronite schools, often supported by missionaries, became centers of learning, producing a class of educated elites who would later lead in politics and commerce. The French connection also gave them a voice in international affairs, for the fate of the Maronites could be raised in Paris as a matter of policy.

But the costs were real. The closer the Maronites aligned with France, the more they appeared to their neighbors as a foreign-backed community, not simply one of Lebanon's own. Their privileges, visible in schools, missions, and later in positions of governance, sowed resentment. The Druze, once equal partners in the mountains, increasingly saw the Maronites as rivals backed by Europe. Muslims, bound by loyalty to the Ottomans, viewed them with suspicion as agents of a foreign power.

By the nineteenth century, these tensions exploded. The 1860 civil conflict between Druze and Maronites left thousands dead and entire villages destroyed. The violence was not only a product of local rivalries but also of the broader struggle between declining Ottoman authority and rising European intervention. France intervened militarily to protect the Maronites, and from that moment, the community's fate was tied even more tightly to the West. What had begun as survival under Ottoman tolerance had turned into open dependence on foreign powers.

The twilight of Ottoman rule brought no relief. The empire was collapsing, European ambitions were rising, and sectarian divisions deepened. The Maronites, once a mountain refuge community, had become a political force leveraged by outsiders. Their endurance was never in question, but their independence was increasingly compromised. They had learned to maneuver within empire, but as the Ottomans faltered, they found themselves exposed, privileged, yes, but also isolated, their future bound not to their neighbors but to powers across the sea.

This precarious balance set the stage for what would come next. The collapse of the Ottoman Empire after the First World War, and the creation of Greater Lebanon under French mandate, would give the Maronites the presidency, the privileges of state, and a chance to shape Lebanon itself. But the roots of both their rise and their fall lay in the centuries of Ottoman rule, where survival was achieved through endurance at home and patronage abroad.

The French Mandate and Greater Lebanon

The collapse of the Ottoman Empire after the First World War reshaped the entire Middle East. New borders were drawn by foreign hands, new states were created where none had existed, and European powers imposed mandates that gave them control under the guise of guardianship. For Lebanon, this meant France. For the Maronites, it meant their long-cherished alliance with the West was finally rewarded.

In 1920, at the behest of Maronite Patriarch Elias Peter Hoayek, first collaborator with foreign power, France proclaimed the creation of Greater Lebanon, carving it out of the old Ottoman provinces. This new entity included Mount Lebanon, the Maronites' historic stronghold, but also Muslim regions that had not been part of their community life: the Bekaa Valley, Tripoli, Sidon, and the south. It was, from the beginning, an artificial construction designed to give the Maronites a state in which they would hold the upper hand. France did not disguise its intent. It saw the Maronites as natural allies, Christian partners who could secure French influence in a region dominated by Muslims.

The new state gave the Maronites unprecedented privileges. They were granted the presidency, the highest office in the land, a position reserved exclusively for a Maronite under the unwritten rules that followed. French advisors and missionaries helped them establish schools, hospitals, and banks. Beirut blossomed as a Mediterranean capital, and Maronite elites were at the center of its growth. For the first time, the Maronites were no longer a mountain refuge; they were rulers of a state.

But this privilege came at a cost. The Muslims of Lebanon, Sunnis, Shia, and Druze, viewed the creation of Greater Lebanon with suspicion or outright hostility. Many Sunnis wished to be part of Syria rather than a French-made state where they were minorities. The Shia, long marginalized, saw no benefit in a system that privileged Maronite elites. Even within the Christian fold, not all were convinced: Greek Orthodox and other sects sometimes resented the Maronites' elevation by foreign powers.

The French Mandate reinforced the Maronites' dependence on outsiders. Their schools and universities, were often run by Jesuit and missionary orders. Their hospitals were funded by French Catholic institutions. Their banking sector was modeled after European systems, structured to serve elites and foreign investors as much as Lebanese citizens. This gave them prestige, but it also meant that their success was tied to the fortunes of Europe, not to the strength of Lebanon itself.

The Maronite leadership embraced this role. Presidents like Charles Debbas (though Greek Orthodox, chosen under French oversight) and later Bechara El Khoury and Camille Chamoun positioned Lebanon as a bridge between East and West, a Christian-led republic that could attract Western investment and protect Western interests. But beneath this façade, divisions simmered. The Maronites celebrated their new state as the realization of a dream, while their Muslim neighbors often saw it as a betrayal, a creation imposed by colonial powers to privilege one sect at the expense of all others.

The French Mandate also deepened the myths that the Maronites had long cultivated. The narrative of Phoenician descent gained even more prominence, reinforced in school textbooks and political speeches. To be Phoenician, they argued, was to be connected to Europe, to trade, to civilization. To be Arab was to be bound to decline and chaos. This framing appealed to French sensibilities but alienated their Arab neighbors, widening the gap between the Maronites and the rest of Lebanon's population.

When France finally withdrew in 1943, Lebanon's independence was born under the shadow of these contradictions. The National Pact, an unwritten agreement between Maronite and Sunni leaders, established that the president would always be Maronite, the prime minister Sunni, and the speaker of parliament Shia. On paper, it looked like compromise. In reality, it entrenched privilege. The Maronites had secured the presidency for themselves, the office that symbolized the state. For decades, this pact would define Lebanon, giving the Maronites dominance but sowing the seeds of resentment that would later tear the country apart.

The French Mandate gave the Maronites their greatest triumph: the state of Lebanon itself. But it also locked them into a system built on privilege, dependence, and fragile bargains. The very power they celebrated would become the burden they could not sustain.

The National Pact: Privilege in Stone

Lebanon's independence in 1943 came not from revolution but from negotiation. The French Mandate collapsed under the weight of global war, and Lebanese leaders seized the chance to define their own political system. But independence was not a clean break; it was an arrangement, a bargain designed to balance communities that mistrusted one another. Out of this bargain came the National Pact, an unwritten agreement that would define Lebanon for decades and carve privilege into its very foundation.

The pact was made between Maronite and Sunni leaders. On the Maronite side, President Bechara El Khoury and his allies sought to ensure that their community's dominance would not be questioned. On the Sunni side, Riad Al-Solh and others sought recognition of Lebanon's Arab identity, resisting the Maronite vision of Lebanon as a purely Western, Phoenician enclave. The agreement that emerged was simple but far-reaching. Lebanon would not seek union with the Arab world, as many Sunnis had wanted, nor would it tie itself exclusively to the West, as some Maronites preferred. Instead, Lebanon would be "with its Arab face," a bridge between worlds.

The distribution of power reflected this compromise. The presidency, the most powerful office, was reserved for a Maronite. The prime ministership was assigned to a Sunni. The speakership of parliament went to a Shia. Other positions were divided among sects, each allocated according to a formula of representation. This system, presented as balance, was in fact hierarchy. The Maronites secured the top office, the symbol of sovereignty, the position from which the state itself spoke. Their privilege was now written into the DNA of Lebanon, not by law but by convention so strong it carried the weight of law.

For the Maronites, this was a triumph. After centuries of refuge in the mountains, after decades of reliance on France, they now stood as the official leaders of an independent state. The presidency was theirs, and with it came the aura of legitimacy and power. Maronite elites flourished, expanding schools, universities, banks, and political networks. Beirut grew into a cosmopolitan city, often described as the "Paris of the

Middle East," and Maronites were at the center of its life.

But this privilege carried a dangerous illusion. It gave the Maronites a sense of permanence, as though their dominance was natural and eternal. It blinded them to the resentments of others. The Sunnis, though given the premiership, often felt sidelined, their influence checked by a presidency that outweighed their role. The Shia, given the speakership of parliament, held little real power and remained marginalized, their regions underdeveloped and neglected. The Druze, once powerful rivals in the mountains, were pushed aside in a system that gave them no guaranteed share.

The National Pact institutionalized sectarianism rather than overcoming it. It told every Lebanese citizen not that they were equal under the republic, but that their fate was tied to their sect. For the Maronites, it seemed like security. For everyone else, it was inequality dressed as compromise.

Over the years, this arrangement hardened into privilege that the Maronites defended fiercely. Presidents like Camille Chamoun and Fuad Chehab used their office to strengthen state institutions but also to reinforce the Maronite place at the top. The church remained a powerful ally, blessing the system that kept the community at the center of national life. But with each passing year, the gap between Maronite privilege and the frustrations of others grew wider.

The pact that was meant to secure Lebanon's independence had, in fact, secured a fragile hierarchy. It gave the Maronites more than their numbers justified, more than history entitled them to, more than their neighbors would indefinitely tolerate. It placed them at the head of the republic but also in the crosshairs of resentment. What they saw as triumph, others saw as imbalance.

The National Pact was not merely an agreement; it was a stone placed in Lebanon's foundation. But it was a stone that carried cracks. The Maronites believed it secured their dominance. In truth, it sowed the seeds of conflict that would later engulf them.

Families, Dynasties, and Parties

The story of the Maronites is not only the story of a community or a church; it is also the story of families. In Lebanon, politics has always been dynastic, and for the Maronites, certain names became synonymous with power, influence, and ambition. These families turned the privileges of the National Pact into private empires, shaping not just Maronite life but the fate of the entire nation.

From the early days of independence, Maronite politics revolved around great houses. The Chamoun family, with Camille Chamoun at its head, built a dynasty that positioned itself as both nationalist and fiercely pro-Western. His presidency in the 1950s aligned Lebanon closely with Western powers, deepening the Maronites' image as guardians of a Christian republic tied to Europe and America. The Frangieh family, rooted in Zgharta, represented another branch of Maronite leadership, traditional, tied to the northern clans, and willing to strike deals with Syria and other forces when it served their interests.

The Gemayel family rose as perhaps the most emblematic of Maronite dynasties. Pierre Gemayel founded the Kataeb Party, also known as the Phalange, a Maronite political force modeled in part on European nationalist movements of the 1930s. Under his leadership, the party grew into one of the most powerful in Lebanon, combining paramilitary strength with political influence. His sons, Bachir and Amine Gemayel, carried the family's ambition further. Bachir, charismatic and ruthless, briefly became president before his assassination in 1982. Amine served as president during some of Lebanon's most turbulent years, embodying both the heights and the vulnerabilities of Maronite politics.

Alongside them, other names carried weight: the Eddé family, with Raymond Eddé known as the "conscience of Lebanon," often standing apart from the corruption and violence of others; the Shihab family, with Fuad Chehab as president, remembered for his attempts to strengthen state institutions and modernize the republic; and the Khourys, with Bechara El Khoury as the first president of independent Lebanon, whose legacy was clouded by corruption.

These families did more than compete; they fractured the Maronites themselves. Each dynasty built its own networks of patronage, its own alliances with foreign powers, its own militias in times of war. Instead of uniting around a shared vision, they divided the community into rival camps. One family leaned West, another leaned toward Syria, a third struck deals with Israel. In this way, the Maronites became not one political force but many, each loyal to a name more than to a cause.

Political parties grew out of these dynasties, but they were never truly separate from family leadership. The Kataeb Party was Gemayel; the National Liberal Party was Chamoun; the Marada Movement was Frangieh. These parties commanded loyalty not just through ideology but through blood, clan, and fear. They mobilized militias when needed, controlled neighborhoods and villages, and extended their influence into the army and state institutions.

This dynastic politics gave the Maronites strength but also fragility. It allowed them to dominate Lebanon's political life for decades, but it also ensured that their community was never united. When crises came,

Maronite leaders often fought one another as fiercely as they fought outsiders. This internal rivalry weakened their position and made them vulnerable to manipulation by foreign powers.

The dominance of families and parties also deepened corruption. Politics became a tool of enrichment, public institutions were carved into fiefdoms, and the state was weakened by endless patronage. For ordinary Maronites, loyalty to a family or party was often the only way to secure jobs, protection, or advancement. The system sustained itself, but at the cost of eroding the very foundations of the republic.

By the mid-twentieth century, the Maronites had achieved what seemed like total dominance: the presidency, the army command, the banks, the universities, and the most powerful political parties. Yet beneath the surface, their community was divided into dynastic camps, each pursuing its own ambition. What looked like unity from outside was, in truth, a patchwork of rivalries. And when Lebanon descended into civil war, these rivalries would prove disastrous, for the Maronites would turn their weapons not only against their neighbors but against each other.

Emile Lahoud: The Exception

President Emile Lahoud was not the first Maronite to hold the presidency of Lebanon, but his name would forever carry a distinction that most of his predecessors and successors could not claim: he aligned himself with the struggle for national dignity. Unlike the political dynasties that trafficked in sectarian power and Western patronage, Lahoud came from a different mold, one carved in the ranks of the military and shaped by a family that valued service above privilege.

Born in 1936 in Baabdat, Mount Lebanon, Lahoud was the son of Jamil Lahoud, a decorated officer in the Lebanese army and a hero of the independence era. General Jamil Lahoud had once served in the French-officered Troupes Spéciales du Levant but joined the nationalist officers who helped rid Lebanon of French control. His father's example imprinted on the young Emile a lasting conviction: the army was the one institution that could serve all Lebanese, above sect and above privilege. This was no small belief in a land where every command and appointment was weighed through the lens of sectarian entitlement.

Lahoud entered the military academy in 1956 and pursued further naval training in the United Kingdom and the United States. This gave him discipline and technical skill, but never bent him toward dependency on Western capitals. By the late 1980s, he had risen through the ranks at a time when Lebanon was still reeling from civil war, the Israeli invasion of 1982, and the continuing occupation of the south.

In November 1989, as the Taif Agreement sought to end the civil war, Lahoud was appointed commander of the Lebanese Armed Forces. The army was fractured, distrusted, and humiliated by years of militia dominance. Lahoud began the slow process of reestablishing professionalism, discipline, and merit. He insisted the army be national, not Maronite, Sunni, Shia, or Druze, if it was to regain any legitimacy.

This vision followed him to Baabda Palace in 1998. Lahoud assumed the presidency not as a backroom politician from Beirut's dynasties but as a general who had lived his career in uniform. He carried little of the orator's charisma, but he held the credibility of a man who had served, not schemed. Many expected him to fall in line with the old Maronite tradition of privilege and Western alignment. Instead, he took a different course.

It was during his presidency that one of Lebanon's greatest national moments unfolded. On May 25, 2000, Israel withdrew from southern Lebanon after twenty-two years of occupation. It was not the fruit of negotiations or international mediation, but the direct result of armed resistance led by Hezbollah and supported by the Shia communities of the south and the Bekaa. For the first time in the Arab-Israeli conflict, Israel retreated without peace treaties, concessions, or recognition. The withdrawal electrified the Arab world.

For many Maronite leaders, this victory was unsettling. Hezbollah's triumph threatened their long-standing narrative of Lebanon as a Christian-led state under Western guarantees. The balance of power had shifted visibly. Yet in Baabda Palace, Emile Lahoud embraced the moment. He declared May 25 a national holiday, "Resistance and Liberation Day," and in doing so validated the Shia struggle in a way no other Maronite president had dared.

This stance came at a cost. The United States and France had hoped Lahoud would serve as a counterweight to Hezbollah and move Lebanon toward disarmament of the resistance. Instead, he defended Hezbollah's weapons as essential so long as Israel remained a threat. His ties to Syria further angered Washington and Paris, both of which wanted Lebanon to pivot away from Damascus and closer to Western influence. To them, Lahoud was the wrong kind of Maronite: not pliant, not useful, not willing to weaken the one force that had liberated Lebanese land.

His presidency was also defined by a fierce rivalry

with Prime Minister Rafic Hariri. Hariri, the Sunni billionaire with deep ties to Saudi Arabia and the West, envisioned Lebanon as a hub of reconstruction, privatization, and global capital. Lahoud, shaped by the army and loyalty to sovereignty, insisted that security and resistance came first. Their rivalry paralyzed governance but also laid bare Lebanon's deeper fault lines: Hariri's Lebanon of Western finance against Lahoud's Lebanon of dignity and defense.

By 2004, the West's frustration with Lahoud was translated into UN Security Council Resolution 1559, which called for Syria's withdrawal from Lebanon and for Hezbollah's disarmament. Lahoud opposed it, and his term was controversially extended with Syrian support, further alienating Western capitals. To his critics, he had become an obstacle to reform and an enabler of Syrian dominance. To his supporters, he was a patriot who refused to bow to dictates written in Washington, Paris, or Tel Aviv.

Among the Shia especially, Lahoud earned enduring respect. While he did not succeed in reforming Lebanon's corrupt political system, he refused to betray the cause of resistance. Unlike Maronite leaders who had collaborated with Israel or sought Western patronage at the expense of national dignity, Lahoud's record stood apart. He became the Maronite president who sided with the oppressed, recognized the sacrifices of the south, and honored the role of Hezbollah when others sought to delegitimize it.

His legacy is complex, as history often is. He could not transcend the Syrian shadow or deliver major economic reforms. But above all, he proved that Maronite leadership did not have to mean betrayal. It could, in rare cases, mean solidarity, humility, and a defense of the nation's honor. His presidency was imperfect, but his refusal to use the office for foreign designs made him a rare exception in Lebanon's modern history.

History tends to classify leaders into patterns. The

Maronite presidency has long been remembered as the office of privilege, designed to secure Western projects at the expense of others. Emile Lahoud broke that mold, if only briefly. His years in Baabda Palace proved that a Maronite president could stand with the Shia, resist Western pressure, and align with Lebanon's dignity rather than its division. His story also poses a haunting question: why was he the exception and not the rule?

Civil War and Collaboration

By the mid-1970s, Lebanon's fragile balance had collapsed. Sectarian tensions, Palestinian militancy, regional rivalries, and economic strain all converged to ignite a war that would last fifteen years. At its heart, the Lebanese Civil War was not just a battle between communities but a reckoning with the system built by the National Pact, a system that privileged the Maronites beyond their numbers and alienated too many of their neighbors. When war came, the Maronites were both defenders of the state and actors in its destruction.

The Maronite political parties transformed themselves into militias almost overnight. The Kataeb Party, led by the Gemayels, fielded the Phalangist forces, a well-armed militia that quickly became one of the most powerful on the Christian side. The Chamouns built the Tigers militia, and the Frangiehs controlled the Marada. These militias claimed to defend the Christian heartland, but they also fought each other for dominance, turning Maronite against Maronite even as they faced external threats.

The war began as a clash between Maronites and Palestinians, whose armed presence in Lebanon had grown after the expulsion from Jordan in 1970. The Maronites feared the Palestinian Liberation Organization (PLO) would turn Lebanon into a battlefield against Israel and upset the country's sectarian balance. The Phalangists, in particular, launched attacks that triggered spiraling violence. The civil war soon widened into a conflict that engulfed every community and drew in foreign armies.

As the conflict deepened, Maronite leaders turned increasingly to outside powers. Some sought Syrian support, others leaned on Israel, and many maintained their ties to France and the United States. This search for patrons was not new, it echoed centuries of dependence, but in the context of civil war, it became collaboration. The most notorious of these alliances came in 1982, when Israel invaded Lebanon. Bachir Gemayel, the charismatic Phalangist commander, was elected president with Israeli backing. His assassination weeks later triggered massacres by Phalangist militias in the Palestinian camps of Sabra and Shatila, carried out under Israeli oversight. The images of that atrocity seared Lebanon's memory and stained the Maronite community's reputation, linking them forever to collaboration with a foreign occupier.

But Israel was not their only partner. Other Maronite factions struck deals with Syria, allowing Syrian troops to enter Lebanon under the guise of peacekeeping. Damascus would remain in control of much of Lebanon for decades, its influence entrenched partly through alliances with Maronite clans like the Frangiehs. Still others looked to Washington, hoping American intervention would secure a Christian-led Lebanon. Each foreign tie deepened dependence and fractured the Maronites further.

The cost of the war was immense. Tens of thousands of Lebanese died, villages were destroyed, and Beirut itself was divided into sectors of militia rule. The Maronite community, which had entered the war as the dominant power in Lebanon, emerged diminished and divided. Their militias, once hailed as protectors, became symbols of brutality. Their leaders, once seen as statesmen, were remembered as warlords. The alliances they had pursued for security left them with the mark of collaboration.

Perhaps the greatest wound was internal. The Christian militias fought not only Palestinians, Muslims, and Syrians, but each other. Rivalries between the Kataeb, the Tigers, and the Lebanese Forces (a militia that emerged from the Phalangists under Bashir's successors) led to bloodshed within the Maronite heartland. Brothers in faith became enemies in politics. In their scramble for supremacy, Maronite leaders weakened the very community they claimed to defend.

The war ended with the Taif Agreement in 1989, brokered by Arab states and supported by the international community. The agreement reduced the powers of the Maronite presidency, shifting authority toward a more balanced system. For the Maronites, this was the final blow: the office that had symbolized their privilege was cut down, their dominance replaced with a fragile parity. What had been secured in 1943 by the National Pact was undone in 1989 by the reality of war and collapse.

The civil war left scars that have never fully healed. For the Maronites, it was a story of defense and betrayal, of resilience and collaboration. They had fought to preserve Lebanon but in doing so had aligned themselves with powers that destroyed its sovereignty. They had sought to defend their privilege but had lost it in the process. What remained was a community weakened, divided, and marked by the memory of choices that would haunt their legacy.

Taif and the Decline of Dominance

By the late 1980s, Lebanon was exhausted. Fifteen years of civil war had shattered its cities, drained its economy, and eroded the credibility of every political faction. For the Maronites, the war had begun as a struggle to preserve their dominance but had ended in fragmentation, collaboration with outsiders, and deep internal wounds. It was in this state of collapse that Arab mediators, backed by international powers, sought to impose a settlement. The result was the Taif Agreement of 1989, an accord that ended the war but also ended Maronite supremacy.

The Taif Agreement was negotiated in Saudi Arabia, under the auspices of the Arab League and with the heavy influence of the United States and Syria. The symbolism was clear: the future of Lebanon would no longer be decided in the mountains of Mount Lebanon or the corridors of Maronite patriarchs, but in Riyadh, Damascus, and Washington. For a community that had once seen itself as the guardians of Lebanese sovereignty, this was a painful reversal.

The agreement preserved Lebanon's sectarian system but rebalanced it. The presidency remained reserved for a Maronite, but its powers were dramatically reduced. The real authority shifted to the Council of Ministers, headed by the Sunni prime minister, and to the parliament, where the Shia speaker gained new weight. The Maronites, who had once held the decisive office, now found themselves as one player among many. Their privilege, carved into stone by the National Pact of 1943, was broken by Taif.

For the Maronite community, Taif was both humiliation and survival. It stripped them of their dominance, but it also ended a war they could no longer sustain. Their militias were weakened, their population had declined through emigration, and their credibility had been eroded by years of internecine violence and alliances with foreign occupiers. By accepting Taif, they conceded power, but they preserved a place in the system.

The years that followed confirmed their decline. Syrian troops, legitimized by Taif, occupied much of Lebanon, controlling its politics and shaping its leadership. Maronite leaders were forced to navigate

Damascus if they wanted influence. Some, like the Frangiehs, adapted, building ties with Syria that kept them relevant. Others, like the Gemayels and Chamouns, saw their power wane. The Maronite presidency became more ceremonial than decisive, its occupant constrained by new balances and by Syrian oversight.

This decline was not only political. Demographics had shifted. Maronites, once close to half the population, were now outnumbered by Muslims, particularly the Shia, whose birth rates and community networks had strengthened their numbers. Waves of emigration had drained Maronite villages, sending their youth to Europe, the Americas, and Australia. Once the heart of Lebanon, the Maronites were becoming a diaspora as much as a local community.

Culturally, their achievements remained visible. Universities like Saint Joseph and hospitals run by Maronite institutions continued to serve Lebanon. Their intellectuals and writers still shaped the country's image abroad. But politically, they were diminished. Their dreams of being Lebanon's rulers had given way to the reality of being one sect among many.

Taif forced the Maronites to confront a truth they had long resisted: Lebanon was not theirs alone to lead. The state they had claimed as their triumph in 1943 had become a shared republic, one where privilege was diluted, and power was divided. For a people who had once believed themselves the guardians of Lebanon, this was a bitter adjustment.

Yet the decline also carried a lesson. The Maronites had fought too long to preserve a dominance that could not be sustained. By clinging to privilege, they had invited resentment, war, and collapse. By the time Taif arrived, they had little choice but to accept the inevitable. The decline of their dominance was not only imposed from outside; it was the natural consequence of decades of imbalance.

From that moment, the Maronites entered a new chapter of their history. No longer the masters of Lebanon, they were now one voice in a fractured republic. Their future would depend not on privilege carved in stone but on their ability to adapt, to build alliances, and perhaps, to find humility.

Diaspora and Survival

As Lebanon's war dragged on and then staggered into the uneasy peace of the Taif Agreement, the Maronite community faced not only political decline but demographic retreat. What they could not secure in Mount Lebanon, many sought abroad. Emigration, long a feature of Lebanese life, became for the Maronites a defining reality. Their diaspora spread across continents, shaping new lives in faraway lands while leaving behind hollowed villages and weakened institutions at home.

The Maronite migration was not new. Since the nineteenth century, Maronites had left Mount Lebanon for the Americas, seeking opportunity in places like Brazil, Argentina, Mexico, and the United States. Their presence in Africa, particularly West Africa, also grew strong, where Maronite traders and entrepreneurs built commercial networks. But the scale of the exodus in the late twentieth century was unprecedented. Civil war, economic collapse, and political marginalization drove hundreds of thousands to leave. By the 1990s, it was clear that the Maronites were no longer just a Lebanese community; they were a global one.

In Brazil, Maronites became part of one of the largest Lebanese communities in the world, producing business leaders, politicians, and cultural figures. In Mexico, families like the Slims rose to global prominence, with Carlos Slim becoming one of the wealthiest men alive. In the United States, Maronite parishes thrived in cities from Detroit to Los Angeles, their churches serving as anchors for communities seeking to preserve identity. In West Africa, Maronite businessmen became power brokers, their influence stretching into the politics and economies of countries like Ivory Coast and Senegal.

This diaspora was both strength and wound. It gave the Maronites influence far beyond their numbers in Lebanon. It allowed them to survive as a people even as their homeland declined. Their wealth abroad often flowed back into Lebanon, sustaining schools, churches, and hospitals. But it also drained the heart of their community. Villages in Mount Lebanon grew empty, their young gone to seek futures abroad. The demographic balance in Lebanon shifted further against them, with the Shia and Sunnis growing while the Maronites dwindled.

The diaspora also reshaped identity. Abroad, Maronites often emphasized their Lebanese heritage more than their sectarian affiliation, presenting themselves as Lebanese first in lands where religion mattered less than national origin. Yet within their churches, the Maronite liturgy and traditions preserved a distinct identity, tying them back to the mountains they had left behind. This duality, Lebanese in public, Maronite in faith, allowed them to adapt abroad while keeping a thread of continuity.

Back in Lebanon, the diaspora's role was double-edged. Their remittances sustained families and institutions, but their distance also meant they had little stake in reforming the politics of the republic. Many in the diaspora idealized a Lebanon that no longer existed, a Christian-led state they remembered from the mid-twentieth century but which had long since faded. Their nostalgia clashed with the realities faced by those who remained, producing tensions within the community itself.

For the Maronite Church, the diaspora was both challenge and mission. Patriarchs traveled frequently to Latin America, North America, and Africa, consecrating churches and strengthening ties. The church presented itself as a global institution, uniting Maronites wherever they lived. But even with this effort, the fragmentation was real: a community once bound by geography was now scattered across continents, its heart divided between homeland and diaspora.

The Maronites' survival thus took two forms: resilience in Lebanon, and adaptation abroad. At home, they faced declining numbers, diminished power, and a fragile future. Abroad, they flourished in business, politics, and culture, often more secure and prosperous than they had ever been in Mount Lebanon. Yet the question lingered: could a people survive as a nation if its strength lay more in exile than in its homeland?

The diaspora kept the Maronites alive, but it also confirmed their decline in Lebanon. A people that had once claimed dominance in Beirut now found its vitality in São Paulo, Mexico City, and Dearborn.

Their story was no longer only Lebanese; it was global. This survival was real, but it was also a confession: that the homeland alone could not sustain them.

The Banking Mirage

For decades, Lebanon's prosperity was built on an image. Beirut was called the "Switzerland of the Middle East," a hub of banking, trade, and finance. Its banks promised secrecy, stability, and high returns, drawing in capital from across the Arab world and beyond. Behind this glittering façade stood many Maronite bankers and elites, who played central roles in shaping and profiting from the system. But the system was fragile, built less on production and industry than on speculation and foreign deposits. When it collapsed, it revealed itself for what it had always been: a mirage.

The roots of Lebanon's banking power went back to the French Mandate, when European financial models were transplanted into Beirut. Maronite elites, with their ties to Paris and Western capitals, became natural custodians of this system. They built banks that catered not to farmers or laborers but to wealthy clients, expatriates, and Gulf investors. Banking secrecy, enshrined in law in 1956, made Lebanon attractive for those seeking to shield wealth from scrutiny. The country became a safe haven for fortunes, a place where oil money, political funds, and hidden assets could rest.

For a time, this model seemed successful. Remittances from the diaspora poured in. Arab elites deposited their money in Beirut. The Lebanese pound was stable, and bankers promised that the state and its currency would never fail. Maronite leaders pointed to the system as proof of Lebanon's exceptionalism, a small country that could thrive on services and finance rather than oil or industry.

But beneath the surface, the structure was unsound. The economy produced little of its own. Banks grew fat on deposits, but these deposits were recycled into government debt rather than investment in infrastructure or development. The state borrowed heavily, and the banks collected interest, enriching their owners while piling up obligations the government could not meet. It was, in essence, a Ponzi scheme: new deposits paid for old debts, and the illusion of stability depended on constant inflows of capital.

When regional crises struck, wars in the Middle East, political instability at home, capital flight shook the system. Yet the bankers reassured their clients, promising that Lebanon's unique model would endure. Among the most infamous figures was Riad Salameh, the long-serving central bank governor, a Maronite who became the architect and defender of Lebanon's monetary policy. For years, Salameh was celebrated as a financial wizard, keeping the pound pegged and the banks afloat. But his policies masked a growing disaster. By offering high interest rates to attract deposits, he created a cycle that only deepened dependence on inflows that could not last.

When the global financial winds shifted and domestic corruption deepened, the scheme unraveled. By 2019, Lebanon's banking sector collapsed, wiping out the savings of millions of ordinary citizens. Families who had trusted banks for generations found their accounts frozen, their dollars vanished, their livelihoods destroyed. The wealthy, including political elites, had already moved much of their money abroad. The burden of the collapse fell not on those who designed the system but on the ordinary Lebanese, Christian and Muslim alike.

The collapse exposed the rot at the heart of Lebanon's postwar order. Banks, politicians, and sectarian leaders had colluded to sustain an illusion that served them while impoverishing the many. For the Maronite community, this was particularly bitter. Many of the faces associated with the system, bankers, governors, ministers, were Maronites, and the community's historic link to finance tied its name to the disaster. What had once been a source of pride became a mark of shame.

The banking mirage revealed the truth: Lebanon's economy had been built not on productivity but on privilege, not on shared prosperity but on elite enrichment. The Maronites, once its champions, now shared in the blame for its collapse. And with the fall of the banks went much of their remaining credibility.

The promise of Beirut as Switzerland was gone. In its place lay a bankrupt state, a broken currency, and a people betrayed. The Maronites, who had once been the guardians of the republic's image of prosperity, now faced the reality that the system they helped build had crumbled into dust.

Achievements and Contradictions

The history of the Maronites in Lebanon cannot be told only as a story of privilege and collapse. Alongside their failures and betrayals stand real achievements that shaped the country and gave it distinction. These achievements, however, carry contradictions that reveal both the community's strengths and its flaws.

The Maronites were central to Lebanon's reputation as a place of learning. With French backing and missionary networks, they built schools and universities that became among the finest in the region. Saint Joseph University in Beirut, founded by Jesuits, trained generations of doctors, lawyers, and intellectuals. The Collège Notre-Dame de Jamhour and other elite institutions gave Lebanon a class of graduates who would serve in leadership positions at home and abroad. The Maronite role in education elevated the country's profile, making it a center of knowledge in the Arab world. Yet this achievement also carried an elitist edge: these schools often served the privileged few, not the struggling many. They opened doors for some, but they reinforced barriers for others.

In healthcare, the Maronite institutions shone as well. Hospitals such as Hôtel-Dieu de France provided modern medical care long before many of Lebanon's neighbors had similar facilities. The Maronite church and charitable orders extended services to villages and towns, ensuring that their community, and often others, had access to treatment. But here, too, contradiction lurked. Many of these institutions were sustained by Western support, not by Lebanon's own resources. Their strength reflected foreign patronage as much as local initiative. What appeared as Maronite generosity was, in truth, another form of dependence.

Culturally, the Maronites contributed richly to Lebanon's identity. Writers, poets, and journalists from the community helped shape Arab intellectual life. Gibran Khalil Gibran, though living much of his life abroad, gave Lebanon a global literary voice. Others, less known internationally but deeply influential locally, worked to build a press and publishing industry that made Beirut the cultural capital of the Arab world for much of the twentieth century. Yet even this cultural flourishing was marked by division. While Maronites celebrated Phoenician heritage and leaned toward the West, their Arab neighbors often viewed this identity as alien, even arrogant. Their art and literature bridged worlds but also highlighted fractures.

Economically, Maronites were pioneers in finance and trade. They built banks, shipping companies, and commercial enterprises that connected Lebanon to global markets. They helped make Beirut a hub for business and investment. Yet their dominance in these sectors reinforced resentment, for others saw them as gatekeepers of privilege rather than partners in growth. The same banks that once gave Lebanon prestige later betrayed it, and the Maronites' association with them darkened their reputation.

Politically, Maronite leaders were instrumental in creating the Lebanese state. They negotiated independence, built institutions, and presided over a republic that, for all its flaws, stood out in a region of monarchies and dictatorships. But the contradictions were stark. Their insistence on privilege alienated others and sowed the seeds of conflict. Their role as builders of the republic cannot be denied, but neither can their role in its unraveling.

The church itself embodies these contradictions. It preserved the Maronite liturgy and culture through centuries of hardship. It gave the community cohesion and resilience. Yet it also tied the Maronites to foreign powers, blessing alliances that deepened dependence. At times it stood with the people; at times it stood with elites. It was both shield and chain.

These achievements and contradictions define the Maronite legacy. They gave Lebanon schools, hospitals, banks, and cultural prestige. But they also gave it divisions, dependence, and illusions. Their story is not one of simple triumph or failure but of both at once, a community capable of greatness yet too often trapped by its own ambitions and fears.

The Maronites cannot be reduced to heroes or villains. They were builders and breakers, visionaries and collaborators, proud custodians of heritage and pawns of foreign powers. Their history is Lebanon's history in miniature: brilliant, tragic, resilient, and flawed.

The glitter of Maronite achievement cannot be separated from the hand that lifted it. Their schools, so often praised as beacons of learning, were founded by Jesuit, Lazarist, and Catholic missionaries backed by France. Saint Joseph University, Collège de la Sagesse, and Collège Notre-Dame de Jamhour stood as symbols of modern education in the Arab East, yet their roots were not purely Lebanese. They were planted by Europeans, nurtured with foreign funds, and designed to extend French influence. Maronite elites embraced these institutions and took pride in their graduates, but the foundation was not theirs alone. Without France, these schools would not have had the reach or prestige they enjoyed.

The same was true of healthcare. Hospitals such as Hôtel-Dieu de France and Saint George's became pillars of modern medicine, providing services that Lebanon's neighbors often lacked. But again, they bore the mark of Europe. Catholic orders supplied doctors, nurses, and funds, while France championed their presence as proof of its protective mission in the East. The Maronites were caretakers and beneficiaries, but the scaffolding was built in Paris and Rome. Their role was to host and to carry the face of institutions that belonged, in truth, to a larger Western design.

Even in banking, the sector that made Beirut the "Switzerland of the Middle East," the model was imported. The 1956 banking secrecy law, often celebrated as a Lebanese innovation, was crafted with the explicit intention of replicating Swiss practices to attract foreign capital. Maronite bankers and elites dominated the industry, but their dominance depended on a system designed for outsiders, Gulf oil wealth, expatriate remittances, and European investors seeking a discreet refuge. The prosperity it created was real, but it was also fragile, tied to global flows they did not control. When the currents shifted, the mirage dissolved.

Politics itself was shaped by the same dynamic. The creation of Greater Lebanon in 1920 was not a Maronite achievement alone. It was the gift of France, carved out of Ottoman lands to reward its Christian allies and secure a colonial foothold. Independence in 1943 was negotiated between Maronite and Sunni leaders, but the framework had already been written by outsiders. The presidency they claimed as their own was not the fruit of self-determination but the product of colonial patronage.

Here lies the core contradiction. The Maronites built schools, hospitals, banks, and a state, but the blueprints came from Europe. Their achievements became the pride of Lebanon, yet they were born of dependence. The Maronites were celebrated as builders, yet too often they were guardians of institutions designed by others. Their strength was real, but it was borrowed.

This truth explains both their prestige and their vulnerability. It gave them tools their neighbors lacked, lifting them for a time above the region. But it also made them pawns in the games of greater powers, praised when useful, abandoned when inconvenient. The same West that once crowned them with privilege would later strip them of protection when Lebanon's balance shifted.

The Maronite legacy, then, is inseparable from this paradox. They stood tallest when Europe held their hand, but their reach faltered when they stood alone. Their story is one of brilliance mixed with dependence, of real achievement overshadowed by the reality that much of it was built on borrowed foundations.

Privileges and Resentments

The Maronites entered Lebanon's modern history with a privilege no other community enjoyed: they were favored by a foreign power that built institutions around them and crowned them as leaders of the state. For decades, they held the presidency, dominated the army command, and filled the ranks of banks, schools, and universities. Their privilege was visible in every corner of Lebanese life, and while they celebrated it as triumph, others experienced it as exclusion.

To the Sunnis, the Maronite claim to privilege was a constant reminder of separation from their Arab environment. Many Sunnis resented that Lebanon had been carved out of Arab Syria by France to serve as a Christian-led enclave. They saw Maronite privilege not as earned but as imposed, a structure built to keep them subordinate in their own land. The National Pact of 1943, though presented as compromise, deepened this resentment by giving the presidency, the most powerful position, to a Maronite, locking in a hierarchy disguised as balance.

The Shia bore an even heavier burden. Long neglected under Ottoman rule, they hoped independence would bring inclusion. Instead, they were left with the weakest position in the pact: the speakership of parliament, a symbolic role with little real power. Their regions, from the Bekaa Valley to the south, remained poor and underdeveloped while Maronite areas flourished with schools and hospitals. To the Shia, the Maronites did not appear as partners but as gatekeepers of privilege who looked down on them as less worthy. This Maronite privilege and exclusion plus the Israeli occupation would, in time, give rise to movements like Amal and Hezbollah, born from resentment of a system that gave them little and took much.

Even among Christians, Maronite privilege caused division. The Greek Orthodox and other Christian sects often resented the way Maronites monopolized representation and claimed Lebanon as their own creation. They, too, had deep roots in the land, yet they were treated as junior partners in a state built around the Maronite presidency and the Maronite Church's alliance with France.

The resentment was not only political but social. Maronite elites controlled the banks and much of the economy, and their wealth stood in stark contrast to the poverty of others. Their ties to Europe allowed them to travel, to study abroad, and to return with advantages unavailable to their neighbors. This produced an image of arrogance, of a community that believed itself more civilized, more Western, and more entitled. For those left out, it confirmed the perception that Maronite privilege was undeserved, a gift of colonial favoritism rather than the fruit of struggle.

Over time, these resentments hardened into hostility. The civil war was not only a clash of armies but a reckoning with privilege. The militias that rose against the Maronites carried with them the anger of decades of exclusion. The Shia who fought for recognition, the Sunnis who demanded Arab identity, the Druze who resisted Maronite dominance, all were reacting to a system that had privileged one community above all others.

The Maronites themselves often failed to see this. From their perspective, their achievements justified their position. They had built schools, hospitals, and banks; they had negotiated independence; they had preserved Lebanon's distinct identity in a region of larger powers. To them, privilege was not a gift but a responsibility they had carried. Yet to their neighbors, it was injustice.

This dual perception, pride on one side, resentment on the other, defined Lebanon's fragile state. It explains why alliances shifted, why trust never deepened, and why every crisis exposed the fault lines anew. The Maronites, convinced of their historic role, could not grasp the depth of bitterness their dominance had produced. Others, consumed by resentment, could not see the achievements that had lifted Lebanon above its region, however unevenly.

The tragedy of Lebanon lies in this divide. Privilege blinded the Maronites, resentment hardened their neighbors, and between them, the republic faltered. What had been presented as balance was, in truth, imbalance. What had been called compromise was, in reality, hierarchy. And when the balance finally shifted, when demographics changed, when war broke their dominance, when Taif stripped the presidency of its power, the Maronites discovered that privilege without humility is unsustainable. Resentment had been growing all along, and when it burst, it washed away the very foundations of their dominance.

Betrayal to Self

In the great traditions of faith, betrayal often begins not with an enemy but with the self. When God created humanity, the angels bowed in reverence, but Iblis refused. In his pride, he declared, *"I am better than him."* In the Western tradition, Lucifer carried the same arrogance, defying heaven itself because he could not accept that another could serve God in ways he would not. The Maronites, in their long history, have carried a shadow of that same defiance.

They were born of the Arab East, speaking Arabic, praying in a Syriac liturgy, rooted in the soil of the Levant. They were not Phoenicians, though they falsely claimed that title. They were not Europeans, though they adopted French as a second tongue. They were not separate from the Arab world, though they sought to deny it. In their refusal to belong fully, they betrayed themselves. They tried to become everything, Phoenician, Western, exceptional, and ended by becoming estranged from their neighbors and from their own identity.

This estrangement bred arrogance. They clung to underserved privileges that were not earned, built by foreign hands and maintained by foreign powers. They collaborated with Crusaders, with French colonizers, with Israeli occupiers, and today with American patrons. Each alliance gave them temporary strength, but each also deepened the distance between themselves and the land they claimed to defend. Privilege made them blind, arrogance made them fragile, and when the winds shifted, their power collapsed like the banking system they had once celebrated.

The European established Maronite experience in Lebanon failed because it was not built on in humility or partnership. It was built on exclusive privilege and dependence. Like the Zionist experiment in Palestine, sustained by foreign arms and money, it has the markings of an outpost rather than a home. Both were crafted by Western powers to serve as posts in the newly divided Middle East after the fall of the Ottoman Empire. One was Lebanon, guarded by the

Maronites. The other was Palestine, entrusted to the Zionists. Both were designed to stand apart from their region, and both now stand on fragile ground.

The path ahead is narrow but clear. The Maronites must reconcile with the truth of who they are. They must accept that they are part of the Arab world, that their faith does not exempt them from belonging, and that their survival depends on loyalty to their land and culture. They must see that arrogance leads only to decline, just as it did for Iblis and Lucifer, who fell from privilege into irrelevance.

If they continue to betray themselves, they will face the same fate, from a privileged place at the center of Lebanon to a dwindling minority remembered only in history books. But if they embrace humility, if they shed the illusion of borrowed identities and foreign crowns, they may yet remain a living part of Lebanon's future.

No outpost of privilege, no matter how radiant at its birth, can endure forever. Only a community that belongs, that serves, and that stands with its people will endure. For the Maronites, the choice is theirs: betrayal to self and decline, or humility and renewal.

Toward Unity and Humility

Every community carries the weight of its history, and the Maronites are no exception. For centuries, they fought to survive in the mountains of Lebanon, then rose to privilege under foreign patronage, and finally saw that privilege drained away through war, emigration, and collapse. Their story is filled with achievements, failures, corruption, betrayal, and contradiction, pride and humiliation. But history is not only a record of what has been; it is also a guide to what can still be. For the Maronites, the way forward lies not in clinging to undeserved privilege but in rediscovering humility and seeking unity with the very communities they once held at arm's length.

The truth is that European granted Maronite privilege benefited the few while it harmed the many. Dynastic families and elites grew rich and powerful, while ordinary Maronites saw little of the wealth and even less of the protection they were promised. The banking system collapsed under the weight of corruption, destroying the savings of ordinary citizens while political and financial elites moved their fortunes abroad. The price of privilege was paid not only by Sunnis, Shia, and Druze, but by Maronites themselves, who saw their sons and daughters leave, their villages empty, and their voice in Lebanon diminished.

The way forward must begin with honesty. The Maronites must acknowledge that their early achievements, while real, were sustained and supported by foreign powers to create a foothold in Arab and Muslim land. They must admit that their privileges were out of proportion to their numbers and undeserved in the eyes of many. They must accept that the days of ruling Lebanon as a Christian enclave are over. In their place lies a different opportunity, to stand as equal partners in a country that will only endure if it belongs to all its people.

Unity requires humility. It means working alongside the powerful Shia, the connected Sunnis, the Druze, and others to reform Lebanon's aging and sectarian political system so that no community dominates and none is marginalized. It means turning away from foreign patrons who have long used the Maronites as pawns and turning instead toward the land and culture that has sustained them for centuries. It means that the Maronite Church, with its ill-gotten wealth, which has too often been a broker of privilege, must become a voice of conscience and real and true Christianity, calling not for dominance but for justice and equality.

There is still time. The Maronites remain an essential part of Lebanon's mosaic. Their schools, churches, and diaspora continue to give them influence and resources. But if they continue to cling to illusions of unfounded exceptionalism, they will dwindle further, reduced to a memory of what once was. If they embrace humility, however, they can help build a Lebanon respected by its own people and by foreigners alike, not because it is a protectorate, but because it is a respected sovereign nation that finally stands on its own.

History offers warnings, but it also offers second chances. The Maronites squandered the first by choosing undeserved privilege over partnership. They may yet redeem the second by choosing humility over arrogance, unity over division, and service over domination. Lebanon's future will not be written by one sect alone. But if the Maronites accept their place as partners rather than agents of foreign powers, they can still write themselves into Lebanon survival and its second coming.

Author's Observations

When I set out to write this book, my purpose was to illuminate the stories of Lebanon's communities, each with its history, its achievements, its limitations. I believed that by understanding each group more deeply, Lebanon might one day come to terms with itself. And by understanding the culture of other communities within this nation, the Lebanese will unite to build a united a non-sectarian nation.

What I did not expect was the overwhelming finding I discovered in tracing the Maronite story. I uncovered not simply a history of survival or faith, but a Western project. France, and later other powers, elevated this community, granting it political and institutional dominance at the expense of all others.

The truth is: Lebanon was never designed as a balanced state; it was engineered as a Western foothold, and the Maronites were placed at its center.

The injustice of this arrangement left The Druze, who had given Lebanon valor and independence without true leadership. The Sunnis, who built trade and commerce and tied Lebanon to the Arab world, were constrained. The Shia, the largest community, the backbone of labor, agriculture, and later resistance, their areas lived for decades under central government neglect leading to impoverished community. Even other Christian communities, namely, the Armenians, who brought culture and craft after surviving genocide, were treated as temporary guests rather than equal citizens.

Meanwhile, the Maronites, through the hands of France and Western powers, were granted institutions, the presidency, the army, and the banks. It was not their merit alone but a foreign design that cemented their role. Just as Britain supported Zionists to build an outpost in Palestine, France and the West relied on the Maronites to anchor their presence in Lebanon. Both projects served foreign interests, not the interests of the people of the region, and both generations later left deep open wounds in the region.

I found myself asking: who gave this community the right to claim control over Lebanon's power while others remained underprivileged?

Who allowed such imbalance to define a nation's fate?

To my surprise, it was not the Shia who acted unjustly when power came into their hands. Despite decades of deprivation, when they rose, they did not erase Lebanon's diversity, nor dismantled the Christian presence. Instead, they showed a surprising measure of restraint. And yet, today, the Maronites project, weakened but not collapsed, continue to align with Western interests, even as the Shia face siege, poverty, and sanctions.

These observations left me disillusioned of Lebanon's unity: The Maronites were not simply favored; they were used and abused. A vibrant community with rich culture and resilience was manipulated, turned into an instrument of Western strategy, and in the process betrayed itself and the land it inhabited. The result is a failed project, a Lebanon divided, its people burdened by a system never meant to serve them equally. As I look back on my research, one truth stands clear: Lebanon cannot survive as the stronghold of one community, nor as the outpost of Western powers. Its survival depends on humility, fairness, and unity, a Lebanon made whole by all its people, not fractured by the privilege of a few.

References

Recommended Readings

Azhari, T. (2020, December 21). *Lebanon's financial collapse: A Ponzi scheme of historic proportions.* Al Jazeera. https://www.aljazeera.com/economy/2020/12/21/lebanons-financial-collapse-a-ponzi-scheme-of-historic-proportions

Baumann, H. (2019). *Citizen Hariri: Lebanon's neoliberal reconstruction.* Oxford University Press.

Britannica. (2025). *Maronite Church.* In *Encyclopaedia Britannica Online.*

Brock, S. (2019). The Syriac Churches: Their early history, literature and theology. In *The Syriac World.* Routledge.

El-Khazen, F. (2000). *The breakdown of the state in Lebanon, 1967–1976.* Harvard University Press.

Hourani, A. (2013). *A history of the Arab peoples* (Updated ed.). Belknap Press of Harvard University Press.

International Monetary Fund. (2022, April). *Lebanon: Staff concluding statement of the 2022 Article IV mission.* IMF. https://www.imf.org/en/News/Articles/2022/04/07/mcs472 2-lebanon-staff-concluding-statement-of-the-2022-article-iv-mission

Makdisi, U. (2000). *The culture of sectarianism: Community, history, and violence in nineteenth-century Ottoman Lebanon.* University of California Press.

Moosa, M. (1986). *The Maronites in History.* Syracuse University Press.

Picard, E. (2002). *Lebanon: A shattered country* (2nd ed.). Holmes & Meier.

Pope Hormisdas. (518, February 10). Letter to the monks of Saint Maron. In G. D. Mansi (Ed.), *Sacrorum Conciliorum Nova et Amplissima Collectio* (Vol. 8).

Saidi, N. (2021, October). *Lebanon's financial crisis: Causes, consequences, and recovery options.* Carnegie Middle East Center. https://carnegie-mec.org/2021/10/12/lebanon-s-financial-crisis-causes-consequences-and-recovery-options-pub-85593

Salibi, K. (1988). *A house of many mansions: The history of Lebanon reconsidered.* University of California Press.

Theodoret of Cyrrhus. (c. 440). *Historia Religiosa (A History of the Monks of Syria).*

Traboulsi, F. (2012). *A history of modern Lebanon* (2nd ed.). Pluto Press.

United Nations Economic and Social Commission for Western Asia. (2020). *Poverty in Lebanon: Solidarity is vital to address the impact of multiple overlapping shocks.* UN ESCWA. https://www.unescwa.org/publications/poverty-lebanon-2020

Zahar, M.-J. (2005). *Power sharing in Lebanon: Foreign protectors, domestic peace, and democratic failure.* In D. Roeder & D. Rothchild (Eds.), *Sustainable peace: Power and democracy after civil wars* (pp. 219–240). Cornell University Press.

About Dr. Abraham Khoureis, Ph.D.

Dr. Abraham Khoureis, Ph.D., is a multi-talented thought leader, global thinker, author, an award-winning mentor, and advocate for compassionate leadership. He is an adjunct professor who specializes in teaching graduate-level courses in business and management, and organizational behaviors, blending academic theory with real-world management and business practices.

Dr. Khoureis is also a small business owner and holds numerous state certifications and professional designations and licenses, highlighting his multidisciplinary expertise.

He is the creator of the Compassionate Leadership Model and Pyramid, which emphasizes leadership built on self-awareness, mindfulness, and commitment to serving others without expectation of return. This seven-level model pyramid, with "Community" as its fifth level, reflects his vision of leadership that positively impacts the broader community and society.

Moreover, Dr. Khoureis developed the Disability Learning Attainment Model, a framework designed to empower individuals with disabilities through inclusive education, skill-building, and leadership development. His work champions and empowers inclusivity, accessibility, and ethical practices in both education and leadership. He has been published on *Forbes.com, Newsweek.com*, and the distinguished *Leader to Leader Journal*. He was recognized as LinkedIn's Top Leadership and Management Voice, and Thinkers360's Top 50 Voices.

Dr. Abraham's contributions extend to his writings, professional development initiatives, and thought leadership, making him a respected emerging leader in the fields of compassionate leadership, organizational behavior, and human resources development.

Readily accessible at:

DrAbeKhoureis.com - DrAbeBooks.com

Social Media: @DrAbeKhoureis

On Amazon.com, search for

Dr. Abraham Khoureis, Ph.D.

Other Books by Dr. Abraham Khoureis, Ph.D.

The Shia of Lebanon: The Guardians of the Nation. SBN: 978-1-966837-343-3

The Druze of Lebanon. SBN: 978-1-966837-37-4

The Sunnis of Lebanon. SBN: 978-1-966837-38-1

SELF: Introducing The Self Rotating Model. ISBN: 979-8-989521-15-9

The Compassionate Leadership Model and Pyramid. ISBN: 979-8-989521-10-4

For his latest list of published books, visit:

DrAbeBooks.com – Or visit,

Amazon.com, search for Dr. Abraham Khoureis

www.ingramcontent.com/pod-product-compliance
Lightning Source LLC
Chambersburg PA
CBHW051928240626
47153CB00004B/1413